let's ook at opposites

Nicola Tuxworth

Up and down

The opposite of up is down. The opposite of down is up.

Up the steps ...

... down the slide. Whee!

Turn it up ...

... turn it down!

Standing
up ...

... falling down.
Whoops!

On and off

The opposite of on is off. The opposite of off is on.

Coat, hat, scarf, boots and gloves off ...

... coat, hat, scarf, boots and gloves on. Out to play!

On the table ...

... off the table.
Oh dear!

On the chair ...

... off the chair.

In and out

The opposite of in is out. The opposite of out is in.

In the car ...

... out of the car. Is there any petrol left?

In the jar ...

... out of the jar.
Mmm! That tastes nice.

In the pool ...

... out of the pool.

Open and close

The opposite of open is close. The opposite of close is open.

Open the door ...

... close the door. Let's play inside.

Open the book ...

... close
the book.

Open the
lunchbox ...

... close the lunchbox.
Yum, yum!

Big and little

The opposite
of big is little.
The opposite
of little is big.

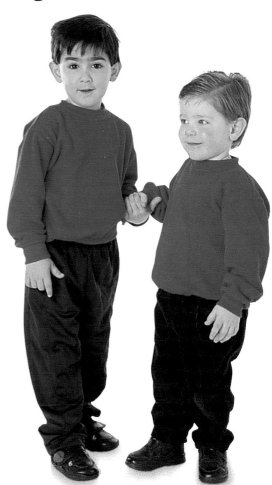

... little brother.

Big ball ...

... little ball.
Catch!

Little
umbrella ...

... big umbrella.
Is it raining?

Big
ice cream ...

... little
ice cream.
Slurp, slurp!

Long and short

The opposite of long is short. The opposite of short is long.

Long sleeves, short trousers ...

... short sleeves, long trousers.

Long, brown hair ...

... short, blonde hair.
Is your hair long
or short?

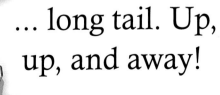

Short
tail ...

... long tail. Up,
up, and away!

Front and back

The opposite of front is back. The opposite of back is front.

Front garden ...

... back garden. Do you have a garden?

Front
pockets ...

... back
pockets.

The front
of a doll ...

... the back
of a doll.

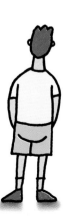

Stop and go

The opposite of stop is go.

The opposite of go is stop.

Stop ...

... Go!
Who will win the race?

Stop ...

... Go! Fetch
the ball!

Stop! The light is red.

Go! The light is green.

Hot and cold

The opposite
of hot is cold.
The opposite
of cold is hot.

Hot weather ...

... cold weather.
Which do you
like best?

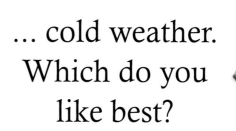

Hot water ...

... cold water.
Brrr!

Hot drink ...

... cold drink.

Awake and asleep

Awake ...

... asleep.
Ssssh!